LITTLE MISS NAUGHTY

and the Fairy Godmother

Roger Hargreaves

Original concept by
Roger Hargreaves

Written and illustrated by
Adam Hargreaves

Little Miss Shy is the shyest person that you will ever meet.

Except that you will probably never meet her because she never goes out.

So she didn't get excited when she received an invitation to Little Miss Splendid's Grand Ball. She got worried and flustered.

She wanted to go.
But she worried about all the people.
So, she would not go.
But she wanted to go.

Little Miss Shy was in a dilemma.

Plucking up all her courage, she rang
Little Miss Sunshine for some advice.

"Do you know what I would do?" said Little Miss
Sunshine. "I'd go out and buy a new pair of shoes.
It always gives my confidence a boost!"

So Little Miss Shy followed her advice and went to
the shoe shop.

"Please, I'd like to buy some new shoes," said Little Miss Shy in a very quiet voice.

"I CAN'T HEAR YOU!" boomed Little Miss Bossy, who worked in the shoe shop. **"SPEAK UP!"**

Little Miss Shy blushed.

"Oooh, look!" cried Little Miss Naughty. "She's turning pink!"

"Good gosh, you're right!" exclaimed Little Miss Bossy.

And she was right. Little Miss Shy was turning pinker and pinker.

"She looks like a strawberry blancmange!" giggled Little Miss Naughty, cruelly.

Little Miss Shy was, by this stage, pink from the top of her head to the tips of her toes. She burst into tears and ran out of the shop.

Poor Little Miss Shy.

She was so miserable she could not sleep.

She sat in front of the fire quietly crying to herself.
"I will never go to the Ball," she sobbed.

"Oh yes you will," came a faraway reply.

Suddenly, a ball of light entered the room and
as it grew brighter, a small, silver-haired woman
appeared at its centre.

"Who are you?" asked Little Miss Shy.

"I am your Fairy Godmother," said the woman, kindly. "And you will go to the Ball."

"But I'm too shy," said Little Miss Shy.

"Not with the right pair of shoes," said the Fairy Godmother, who waved her magic wand.

Little Miss Shy's old bedroom slippers transformed into a pair of glass ballroom slippers.

The most beautiful shoes Little Miss Shy had ever set eyes on.

Then, the most amazing thing happened.

Little Miss Shy was suddenly filled with confidence.
All her shyness disappeared!

"But, you must remember," warned the Fairy Godmother,
"that on the last stroke of midnight on the night of the
Ball, if you are still wearing the shoes, they will turn
back into ordinary bedroom slippers."

The following evening, Little Miss Shy went to the Ball and she had the most wonderful evening of her life.

She danced all night long.

Everyone was dazzled by her beautiful glass slippers.

Little Miss Shy was so unlike her usual self that nobody recognised her.

Near the end of the Ball, Little Miss Splendid stood up and made an announcement.

"I have a surprise for you all. There is a prize for the best dancer at the Ball tonight, and I and my fellow judges have decided that this prize should be awarded to . . . " she paused, ". . . the girl in the glass ballroom slippers!"

As Little Miss Splendid spoke, the bell in the clock tower rang the first stroke of midnight.

In a flash, Little Miss Shy remembered the
Fairy Godmother's warning.

She couldn't go up and receive her prize without the
glass slippers. Little Miss Shy could feel herself starting
to blush. She panicked and fled from the ballroom.

As she ran, one of the glass slippers fell from her foot.

"Where is the girl in the glass ballroom slippers?" called Little Miss Splendid.

But nobody could find her.

She had disappeared.

All they could find was one glass slipper.

"I must have my winner!" cried Little Miss Splendid. "Search the land until you find her!"

So Little Miss Splendid's friends went out in search of a girl whose foot would fit the glass slipper. Everybody wanted to claim the prize, but nobody's foot would fit.

Little Miss Bossy and Little Miss Naughty tried on the slipper and of course it did not fit either of them.

"You should try Little Miss Shy," suggested Little Miss Naughty, slyly.

"Let's go and watch her turn pink," she said to Little Miss Bossy.

"Oooh, you are naughty," giggled Little Miss Bossy.

So they all arrived at Little Miss Shy's house.

Poor Little Miss Shy. She did not know where to put herself.

And of course, she turned pink.

But not as pink as Little Miss Naughty and Little Miss Bossy when the glass slipper fitted Little Miss Shy's foot!

They were speechless!

"Little Miss Splendid will want to present your prize to you in person," said Mr Happy.

Little Miss Shy's prize was a pair of pink dancing shoes.

Her Fairy Godmother smiled down on her as Little Miss Splendid put the shoes on Little Miss Shy's feet.

They fitted perfectly.

And they matched Little Miss Shy perfectly.

Little Miss Shy was very proud and very pink!